Go! Go! Sports Girls™

Soccer Girl Cassie's Story

Teamwork Is the Goal

Written by Kara Douglass Thom

Illustrated by Pamela Seatter

Dream Big Toy Company™

When Cassie met Anna on the school bus, she found her new best friend...and her new favorite sport.

The Name of the Game

Soccer is the most popular sport in the world! But in countries besides the United States, it is usually called football.

Soccer Rules!

There is evidence that soccer was played in the Middle Ages, in places like China and Japan. In 1863, a set of rules for soccer was made in England. Known as "The Laws of the Game," these are the rules we still use today!

4

Each morning, Anna sat down next to Cassie and talked about soccer, all the way to school. Anna's father had been a professional soccer player in Brazil. He had taught Anna how to play.

Cassie had never played soccer before. She loved listening to Anna's stories about soccer practice, and she especially loved hearing about the games.

When spring came, Cassie asked her mom if she could play soccer, too.

Gear Up!
To play soccer, you'll need:
— Shorts and a jersey, or a team uniform
— Socks, shin guards, and gym shoes or cleats
— A soccer ball
— A goal net, or something to mark the goal line.

Cassie's mom said *YES!*

At her first practice, Cassie had a hard time remembering *not* to pick up the ball with her hands. She tripped over the ball when she tried to dribble it down the field. When the coach put Cassie in the net to play goalie, she was afraid of getting hit with the ball.

Most of all, Cassie wondered where Anna was. Playing with her friend was one of the main reasons Cassie signed up for soccer. But she was put on a team named the Shooting Stars, and Anna was on a team named the Sun Dogs.

Hands Off!

Goalies can use their hands, but other players must not let the ball touch them between their fingers and shoulders. In soccer, to "dribble" means to move the ball with your feet.

"Don't worry," Anna told Cassie on the bus the next morning. "We'll get to play soccer together."

"We will?" Cassie asked. "When?"

"When our teams compete against each other."

"Against each other?" Cassie gulped.

Cassie had heard plenty of stories about Anna's soccer games. They always ended the same way: with a win for Anna's team.

Anna played the forward position. She knew how to take control of the soccer ball, dribble it down the field, and score! She could shoot the ball right past the other team's goalie into the net. Anna was a soccer star.

What's the Goal?

During a soccer match, two teams each try to get the soccer ball into the other team's goal. At the same time, they try to protect their own goals so the other team can't score. The team with the most goals at the end of the game wins.

Over the next few weeks, Cassie learned lots of soccer skills. She liked playing forward, just like Anna. It was such a thrill to kick the ball into the net!

But Cassie's coach thought she was a strong defender. She was good at passing the ball to her teammates. And, when the other team had the ball, she was good at keeping them from shooting at her team's goal and scoring.

Who's Who?
These are the main positions on a soccer team.

- A goal keeper, or goalie, tries to keep the ball from crossing the goal line and entering the net.
- Defenders stay by their own goal to stop the other team from scoring.
- A sweeper is a defender who moves through the field behind the other defenders to "sweep up" the ball when her teammates can't get to it.
- A midfielder can defend her goal or move the ball toward the other team's goal.
- Forwards play close to the other team's goal so they can try to score.
- A striker is a forward who makes most of her team's shots.

Finally the day came for the Shooting Stars to play the Sun Dogs. The Sun Dogs were the best team in the league. Anna's dad was the coach, and Anna was their top scorer.

Cassie's coach wanted her to play defense. She knew she would need to stop one player from scoring: Anna!

As Cassie walked toward the soccer field, she saw Anna come running.

"Hi Cassie!" Anna called. She juggled the ball with her knees and feet. "Ready for the game?"

Cassie nodded. But her green eyes darted from her friend down to the grass under her feet. She didn't think she was as ready as Anna.

"My dad says our team gets a pizza party after we win five games," Anna said. "We've won four already, so we're really going to try hard to win today!"

Cassie wanted to win too. But even if the Shooting Stars tried as hard as the Sun Dogs, could they really beat them?

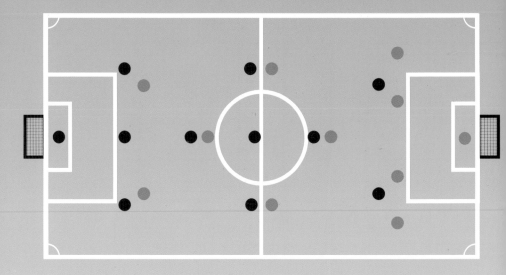

Cassie wasn't sure. But the Shooting Stars had worked hard this season. They were getting better at passing the ball to each other. They remembered to tell each other where they were on the field, and when they were open for a pass. They had already won two games. And they had learned lessons from the games they lost.

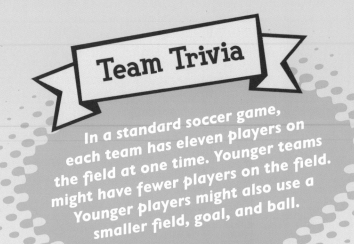

Team Trivia

In a standard soccer game, each team has eleven players on the field at one time. Younger teams might have fewer players on the field. Younger players might also use a smaller field, goal, and ball.

"Well, may the best team win!" said Anna.

"Our coach says that sometimes losing helps you become a better player," Cassie said.

Anna gave Cassie a funny look. Then she ran off to join the other Sun Dogs.

The referee blew his whistle. Game time!

Anna sent the kick-off bouncing to her teammate on the freshly mowed field.

Zip. Zip. Zip.

The ball zigged and zagged from one team to the other.

When Anna got the ball, Cassie sprinted to her side and toe-poked it away. The ball spun loose from Anna's path, and Cassie took it. Just as Anna came back for the ball, Cassie saw another Shooting Star waving at her.

"I'm open!" Cassie's teammate Gracie yelled. Quickly Cassie passed the ball to Gracie. Then Gracie kicked it to Sam, who was closer to the net. Before the Sun Dogs could see that Anna no longer had the ball—score!

The Shooting Stars had their first goal!

Anna looked stunned. She ran alongside Cassie and asked, "You had the ball. Why didn't *you* score the goal?"

"Because Gracie and Sam were closer to the net," Cassie said. "They had a better chance to score than me."

Good Sport

A "good sport" is a player who tries her best to win for her team, and also has good manners on the field. Even though you are competing, you can still respect the other team.

Play Nice!

You might bump into another player when you both go after the ball, but pushing, kicking, tripping, and pulling are against the rules.

After the next kick-off, the ball zigged and zagged until, once again, it met Anna's cleats. Her quick feet dribbled the ball forward. She moved closer and closer to the goal. Then Cassie rushed to Anna's side and blocked her way.

"Here comes my shadow," Anna said.

Anna's teammates were open to her right, to her left, and behind her. But she didn't pass the ball to them. She kept trying to shoot it toward the goal herself—and Cassie kept trying to stop her.

While Anna tried to get a clear shot, Cassie put the sole of her foot on the ball and dragged it out of Anna's reach. Then she quickly turned and passed the ball to another Shooting Star—who scored another goal!

"Yes!" Cassie shouted. She raised her arms high above her head.

"I was so close," Anna said, shaking her head. "I should have scored."

"Maybe if you had passed the ball to one of your teammates..." Cassie started to say, and then stopped. Anna already knew how to play soccer, and she had won a lot more games than Cassie.

Game Time

Standard soccer games have two 45-minute halves, with a 15-minute half-time break. Youth soccer games usually have four 10-minute quarters, or two 20-minute halves.

At half-time, Cassie's coach praised the whole team for working so well together.

"There is no I in TEAM," she said. "You can all take the credit for the two goals we scored."

During the second half of the game, the sun was higher and the day was hotter. Drops of sweat ran down Cassie's cheeks as she followed the ball across the field. The Sun Dogs defended their goal, and the Shooting Stars couldn't get near the net.

As the minutes ticked toward the end of the game, Anna drove the ball down the field again. The Shooting Stars were close behind her. When Cassie came to Anna's side, Anna said, "There's my shadow again!"

Then, to Cassie's surprise, Anna passed the ball to her Sun Dog teammate—who shot the ball into the Shooting Stars' goal in the last seconds of the game.

"That was an awesome play, Anna!" Cassie grabbed her friend's shoulders and smiled. "You didn't kick the ball into the net, but you set up the goal."

Anna looked over at her team. The Sun Dogs were still celebrating their goal, even though they didn't win the game. "It does feel good to make the assist," she said. "Just like your coach said, losing the game made me a better player. Hey, congratulations on your win!"

"Thanks, Anna!" Cassie said. "Your team played a fierce game. Look at me! Your 'shadow' is soaking wet."

Anna smiled. "My shadow," she said, "is turning into a star."

Cassie felt her cheeks turn pink at her friend's compliment. "Hey—I need to cool off," she said. "Do you want to go swimming with me? I told Suzi I might meet her at the pool."

FIELD

POOL

"Do I have a choice?" Anna looked at Cassie with a big grin. "I go wherever my shadow goes!"

31

Here's What Cassie Learned:

- The goal in soccer is teamwork! Teammates need to work together to win.

- Sometimes losing helps you become a better player.

- Learning a new sport can be hard. Just keep trying!

- Be a good sport, no matter what happens on the field. The game will end, but friendships keep going.

Soccer Girl Cassie's Healthy Tips:

- **Warm up.** The Shooting Stars soccer team does jumping jacks and toe-touches before every game.

- **Eat up.** Choose natural snacks like an apple or a handful of almonds. These give you more energy than sugary snacks.

- **Drink up.** Your body loses water when you sweat. Replace it by drinking water, not sodas or sugary drinks.

- **Cover up.** To protect your skin, put on sunscreen whenever you play outdoors.

- **Rest up.** Get lots of sleep every night, especially before games.

Dream Big and Go For It!